THE BLIZZARD'S SECRETS

DJANÉE

Second edition.
First published by DJanée 2023

Editing & Proofreading: Salima Alikhan, Leonora
Bulbeck, Alexandra Ott
Interior Formatting: MiblArt
Cover Design: MiblArt

ISBN: 979-8-9885063-0-0 (paperback)
ISBN: 979-8-9885063-1-7 (epub)
ISBN: 979-8-9885063-2-4 (hardback)

pROLOGUE

I puff hot air into the cold and watch the small cloud dissipate. I take another breath in and release it. Out goes the condensation, before it disappears.

It's cold, and my body shivers and shakes like a leaf trembling in the wind. I try to stop it, but the freezing cold has reached my bones. My hands grip the blanket around me as I huddle by the fire for warmth, my jaw noisily banging my teeth together.

The cave is pretty dark, but the icicles glisten in the dancing light from the flames. They dangle sporadically from the ceiling, but none hang precariously above me. Layers of ice cloak sections of the rocky walls.

The Ruler of our people stands farther toward the mouth of the cave and watches the storm. The loud wind whirls blinding snowflakes in a symphony of death. How can something so beautiful be so dangerous, so lethal?

The Ruler isn't fazed by the frigidity. He has that special blood in him that I wish I had—the warm blood of a direct descendant of our tribal ancestors. They were accustomed to the cold. They wound up migrating from a land like this—of dangerous creatures and treacherous storms—to the place of paradise that our community lives in now: Taliver. They intermingled with the natives of the community and created people like me, who are not so resilient to the cold.

Still, the Ruler wears his heavy brown coat of furs, which hangs down to his knees. He just stands there, staring … just staring … out into the deadly cold.

"We have more wood for the fire," Petrus says. He drops five more logs beside the ones already keeping the fire ablaze.

I look up at his large brown eyes and strong, sharp facial structure. They contradict with one another, bouncing between innocence and maturity. In the end, the contrast manages to blend nicely under his short, dark hair.

Petrus also wears a thick, dark-brown coat of furs down to his knees. He is not as cold as I am either. He's also a direct descendant of our tribal ancestors and a soldier of our community.

I wear moderately warm attire with thick, brown garments, but it's clearly not warm enough. I didn't prepare for this kind of weather. Even if I did, I'm sure I would still be cold, since I'm of mixed descent. The Seer warned me against coming out here. He told me that the weather was treacherous, but I was too stubborn. I believed that I could beat the storm, but he was right. The weather is rougher here than in most regions—certainly rougher than in Taliver.

It tackled me harder than I had anticipated, throwing me several feet and through the ice of a frozen lake. I was fortunate that the Ruler and Petrus had already caught up enough to see what happened and pull me out before any large, fanged aquatic creatures got to me. There are stories … and they tell why we are not supposed to leave the safety of our community.

Remembering the treachery of the howling, dangerous storm outside makes me shudder.

"Oh, whoa," Petrus says. He shakes out another blanket I didn't notice a few yards away.

He swings it around me and drapes it over my shoulders. The warmth manages to mitigate the shivering, removing some of the chill from my bones. I'm grateful for it.

The Ruler glances back from where he stands.

"There." Petrus sounds relieved, noticing my body stilling. He sits on the other side of the fire. "You're fortunate we found you when we did—"

"Fortunate?" the Ruler jumps in.

Petrus and I turn in alarm to look at the Ruler, and he holds our gazes for a moment. He slowly strides over to us, taking heavy, deliberate steps.

"'Fortunate' doesn't even cut it," he says. "You could've been hurt—injured—obliterated. You could have been *killed*!"

His anger is to be expected—even in front of one of my soldiers. To Taliver's subjects, he is the Ruler—always faithful, always true. And I just violated community guidelines despite my looming position as Commander of the Forces, putting my life at risk. Of course the Ruler should be troubled. I had my reasons, though. And the Ruler knows it, although he won't say that in front of Petrus.

"Why would you come out here?" Petrus looks at me with pleading eyes, searching for a reason why his soon-to-be Commander would do something so irresponsible. That's the hard part—seeing that doubt in one of my soldiers, in someone who should be confident in my leadership. But I have to do this for them … even if I can't tell them why yet.

The Ruler interjects. "There is no valid reason for sneaking out of Taliver and defying orders. What you did was foolish and reckless." He glances at Petrus before gazing out at the blizzard, seeming to regain composure for the sake of the respect still owed to my position. "When the morning breaks, we take her back."

Petrus doesn't move.

The Ruler glances at me again, meeting my gaze for a brief moment, before he walks away.

Maybe I went too far. Maybe I shouldn't have wandered into the night in the first place and should have just left things alone. But I didn't have much of a choice. I knew that something was wrong. There are clearly lies and suspicious mysteries within Taliver, and I don't know what they could mean for my people. I have to protect them, but I can't do that unless I know the truth.

I must find the one man who can help me sort it all out. I have to fulfill the mission I was sent on. Little does the Ruler know, I have my own objective. I will uncover the truth, I will protect my fellow citizens, and I will make sure there is justice for my people. That is my duty as the next Commander of the Forces. No, I don't regret coming out and facing the Tundra. But now I have to find a way to sneak out again. The fate of Taliver and its citizens depends on it.

Chapter 1

My name is Daia, and I am
the next Commander of the Forces.

I stare at the line I have written on the paper in front of me on the wooden-plank table. It doesn't feel right. It's too mechanical and impersonal.

I crumple it into a little ball and throw it over my shoulder onto the floor somewhere. There are probably five balls of paper scattered behind me at this point.

In Taliver's castle, I sit in my small study, reserved for me as the next Commander of the Forces and for the Seer. This is where we typically meet for mental preparation and training. The study almost looks like a library, with its tall, overstuffed bookshelves crammed into the little space, meeting in a corner to my left. Books and papers practically hang off the shelves.

An old, beige, fabric couch sits a few feet to my right, facing me and a small wooden coffee table in front of it. A blanket is untidily strewn across the couch, and papers litter the cushions as well as the floor. All along the wall behind me are a couple of standing globes and more unorganized, shorter bookcases and cabinets.

Everything here is really the Seer's. It is more his space than mine, which is why it looks the way it does. I just try to ignore the chaos.

"Have you prepared your speech for the ceremony?" The Seer steps in through the open doorway behind me.

I stare at the blank sheet of paper, acknowledging to myself that I have accomplished absolutely nothing after perhaps an hour of slaving away over this speech for my induction ceremony in two days. After years of training and mental preparation with the Seer, I have been deemed ready to take on the responsibility of leading Taliver's army. Yet I cannot put the right words together for my transition.

"I can't get it right," I tell him, still staring at the paper.

I swivel around on the bench to look at him. He is untidily dressed in a long robe of rust-red and gold. I'm not sure if the gold used to be more vibrant, but it looks like a dull, dim ghost of the color. The belt for his robe is undone, and he wears a white undershirt beneath. He also wears white socks that come up halfway to his knees and bulky black sandals, and his prematurely graying hair is a mess around his head. He holds a mug of coffee. I just catch a scent of it, but it smells overly bitter and like it might be old. He looks right at home, which is fitting, seeing as his residence is just down the hall. But to be honest, his appearance doesn't change much whether he's here in the study or out walking the streets of Taliver among its citizens.

He sits beside me. He carries a faint, damp smell of worn years, which mingles with the strong, bitter coffee.

"Let me hear it—" He stops himself when he sees the blank page on the table. He looks back at the crumpled balls of paper on the floor. "Ah."

"How am I supposed to lead our armed forces when I can't even assemble a speech? What if I'm not really ready for this?" I ask, hoping for some kind of reassurance.

"You're ready," he tells me, almost sounding amused. "The Ruler and I wouldn't have agreed on it if we thought otherwise."

"How do you know?"

His eyes change as he realizes that I am genuinely afraid. I look away, ashamed of my own vulnerability, but I know I have to address this.

"The Commander before me led during a time of peace and wound up assisting the last Ruler in revitalizing the marketplace and maintaining peace in Taliver. The Commander before him led the army to force dangerous creatures back before they got too close and demolished our community. What have I done that shows I'm even *remotely* ready for something like that? And now I'm afraid of a little attention during a ceremony?"

My throat clenches, and my eyes begin to sting. What if dangerous creatures or some foreign community come to invade Taliver, and I don't handle it properly? What if I lead my people to their deaths or don't know what's best for them, even though I may think I do? The lives and the well-being of so many people are in my hands, and I'm starting to wonder if I can protect them.

The Seer takes a deep breath, nodding like he understands. "You know, I had a similar concern when I was inducted as the Seer."

I look at him. "Really?"

He nods. "Yes. I didn't like the spotlight either, and I didn't know if I could live up to the standards of previous Seers."

"What did you do?" I ask.

He takes in another breath. "I … cheated."

My eyebrows fly up.

He presses his lips together and nods again. His eyebrows are furrowed like the memory is tainted by fresh guilt, as though he had done this just yesterday.

"Yeah. I'm not particularly proud of it, but … yes, I cheated."

The Seer? My Seer? Cheated? Admittedly, he's not the most organized person, but his character is far from questionable. For the Seer to do something this controversial, there had to have been something dire at hand, which only piques my curiosity more.

I shape my lips to inquire about what
happened, but I cannot bring the words out. He
already knows, though.

"It was winter ..."

Chapter 2

"It was winter, and I had begun my training with who was then the Seer. Only, he lived out beyond Taliver's defensive wall, about half a day's journey from here, in the Frozen Tundra."

My surprise must be apparent on my face, because the Seer pauses to nod, acknowledging the peculiarity of what he has just said. Citizens are not supposed to go outside the wall of Taliver, let alone *live* outside them. This is to keep everyone safe from treacherous lands that are not too far away, like the Frozen Tundra, where hazardous storms and creatures reside. Only certain personnel can venture outside the wall, and even then, only with proper approval from the Ruler. The restraint on officials, who now require consent before leaving Taliver, was introduced by the current Ruler, being the protective leader that he is. No one really goes out there, anyway—not even the Ruler.

"The weather there is much colder than it is here," the Seer continues, "so I always had to bundle up whenever I went out for our weekly sessions."

He pauses, reminiscing with an amused look on his face.

"Anyway, I visited his house one time. I call it a house, but really, it was more like a small log cabin. I knocked on his door, and he didn't answer.

"Now, I never asked him why he lived out in the Tundra, as I didn't want to be rude or invasive. I was very young—a few years younger than you were when you started, as a matter of fact." He glances at me. "Responsibility began much younger in my generation."

I nod and take notice of how much he interrupts his own story. He tends to do this. Even in his speech, he is not the most orderly person. He is only the Seer for his wisdom—not at all for his organization.

"His absence was abnormal, though," he continues. "I looked in through the windows for any sign of him. It was hard to see because the windows were extremely thick. All I found through those glowing golden panes was a glimpse of a fire burning in a small fireplace and the wooden table and chairs we'd sit at for my lessons. Then I noticed something odd. I could barely see it, but I felt sure that I saw a hand lying on the floor by the table."

I raise my eyebrows in surprise.

"I came back to the door and kicked at it until it swung open. I rushed in and found him lying on the floor on his side. I shook him, trying to wake him, but he wouldn't stir. Above him, still on the table, a mug that he had been drinking from was lying on its side. I sniffed it, finding that it had a foul odor. Now, of course, I have no proof that it was a homicide. The truth is, it could have been a suicide, or maybe the beverage wasn't poisonous at all. I really don't know." He shrugs.

"But wouldn't the officials of Taliver investigating his death have been able to tell if it was a concoction made with a poisonous root?"

"That's just it. I didn't tell anyone."

I look at him in shock. "Why wouldn't you tell anyone?"

He glances down at the floor, almost saddened. "Because he was no longer the Seer. I wasn't supposed to go to him anymore. Something happened where he had to leave Taliver. The Ruler was young at that time as well, and he forbade me from seeing him for my sessions. No one would tell me exactly what happened, but violation of the law would naturally mean a possible sentencing to imprisonment in the dungeon or worse."

I can only presume that the late Seer was exiled from Taliver, but I can't imagine what an official as close and loyal to the Ruler as a Seer could possibly do to warrant exile. I imagine the Seer doing anything remotely treasonous, like murder or leading a rebellion, and it clashes with his character so much it almost makes me cringe. I bring my thoughts back to the Seer's story.

"But you still went to him—your Seer," I conclude.

"Yes. There is only one Seer at any given time, and I didn't think I was ready for the role yet."

"But why would the Ruler forbid you from seeing the only Seer? Where did he expect you to get your training?"

He shrugs. "He didn't. He was going to completely do away with Seers and just have the Ruler select and train those officials who would normally be a Seer's responsibility. You, for instance, would not have been elected as Commander by me and then approved by the Ruler. Rather, the entire decision and training process would have been solely handled by the Ruler."

This seems odd, seeing as the Ruler is already responsible for our people's protection, culture, justice, and everything else that makes Taliver function. Adding the Seer's responsibilities seems peculiar—almost suspicious. However, the Seer was a child at the time. He could have misunderstood something. Furthermore, the Ruler was young as well, and his judgment may not have been as sound as it is today.

Either way, I'm not worried. Clearly, that idea was not put into practice. And I know the Ruler—Julius is his name, though of course, I never call him that, out of respect. Over the years since I entered training to become Commander of the Forces, I've grown rather fond of him. He is passionate about our citizens' well-being and is known for being "always faithful, always true." He is a great leader.

"He saw my progress, though," the Seer continues. "He heard the wisdom I spoke and advised with, and he believed that I was a natural. So ..." He spreads his arms to showcase himself as the present Seer.

"But didn't people notice when you were missing? You said it was half a day's journey."

"People see only what they want to see. The idea of a future Seer within Taliver venturing off into the Tundra to associate with someone who had been exiled was not even conceivable back then. I just misdirected people, saying that I was here or telling others that I was there, and no one bothered to question me. I was very highly respected for my age."

"Well, what does this have to do with my speech and being rea—" I freeze, realizing all that he had to deal with in that scenario. Though he had continued his training, it came to an abrupt halt when his Seer died—before he felt ready to take on the role of Seer. "*You* didn't feel ready for your role when you spoke at your induction ceremony either."

He shakes his head. "Nope, and I did a pretty good job handling all of it, too. Daia ..." He shakes his head. "You *have* that natural sense of wisdom—that ability to rise to the occasion. I've seen your instincts in training, your love for the people, your natural sense of duty, which all surpass anything I could have ever taught you. You're a natural-born *leader*. You're ready. And the mere fact that you are so concerned about the lives that are being placed in your hands just further proves that."

He smiles at me, and with just those words and that simple expression, the anxiety starts to subside. The heavy burden lifts off my shoulders, and I smile back at him, grateful for his influence in my life. He always understands me. And he always knows just what to say—even though I think he plays down the role he's had in cultivating who I am today. I am all those things he mentioned because of him. I don't know where I would be without him.

"So," I say, considering his story, "you don't know what happened to your Seer?"

"Nope," he says, visibly shifting his attention from how proud he is of me. "And I've never been back out there since. I know this, though: whatever happened, it wasn't good."

Chapter 3

"All right, Daia. After this, we have one more session tomorrow before your ceremony. Let's make these sessions count. Focus."

The Seer and I face each other in the study. He extends his hands to me, palms up. I place my hands in his and close my eyes.

"That's it," he encourages. "Relax."

This is an exercise we use to help center my mind and clear my thoughts. We usually do this at the beginning of our sessions. Hopefully, this will help me with my speech, in conjunction with the Seer's encouraging words. I let all my questions about the Seer's instructor melt away from my mind.

I take a deep breath in ... and then let it out slowly ...

Another deep breath in … and then let it out slowly …

Any remaining tension slowly seeps out of me, and my mind grows quieter.

Another deep breath in … and—

The door to the study swings open with a booming whack against the wall, shocking me out of my concentration.

"Head Daia!"

I can almost hear the soldier's immediate regret at having clearly interrupted his leader's session. I may be young and may not yet have taken over as Commander, but I am already respected in my role. And all except the Seer formally address me by my title: Head Daia.

I turn to see Steven, the right-hand man of the Ruler. He's dressed in shining armor and stands in the doorway with apologetically furrowed eyebrows.

"It's all right, Steven," I tell him with a raised hand. "What is it?"

Steven stands at attention, his hand still on the doorknob. "The Ruler wishes to speak with you, Head Daia." He tilts his head down to look at me more directly. "Immediately."

This catches me off-guard, and I look back at the Seer. He appears to be just as surprised and curious as I am. It is rare to be summoned into the Ruler's presence—even for me or the Seer. It is even rarer to be summoned under the order of "immediately."

I look back at Steven. "All right."

He steps aside for me to walk through the doorway as I approach. I spare one more glance back at the Seer's inquisitive face before I step through the door.

The hallway stretches far to the left and right, with brown wainscoting and a gold-trimmed red carpet running through it. Above the wainscoting, paintings of flowers and other beautiful features of nature hang from the walls—along with portraits of significant people from our past.

Across the hallway, not too far from where I stand, hangs a large portrait of the original Ruler of our community—the first to hold the position after our tribal ancestors stumbled upon Taliver. He was a very large man with big, thick fingers. In the portrait, his hair trails down his back in a thick braid according to the tradition of our ancestral tribe. It is the way of powerful men. He also wears an ornate red crown and has a scruffy beard, and he holds a scepter in one hand and a red cushion in the other—all of which are traditions done away with long ago. Rankings and positions are not so flamboyantly and formally displayed now, though there are protocols in place to give honor and respect to officials, such as addressing them by their titles.

Steven comes out behind me and closes the door. "We should hurry, Head Daia." He gestures for me to continue down the hall to the left.

I nod and start walking.

Despite my high placement and my stature within the community, I am in the dark. I cannot help but wonder what this meeting is about and think about what the Seer just told me. His Seer was an outcast for some mysterious reason.

On the same day that he tells me this, I am required to appear "immediately" before the Ruler. And this is all not long before my induction ceremony. I can't help but wonder where all of this is coming from and what connection these events may have to one another. I can't help but feel suspicious of what it all may mean.

Chapter 4

We walk through the hallway in silence, with the exception of Steven's clanking armor. We turn a number of corners until we reach very tall, elegant doors decorated in red-and-gold engravings in a corner of the hallway. Three dragon-head knockers line the height of each door. The top four are too high for me to reach.

I brace my hands against the doors and push against the heavy weight that they carry. They don't budge at first—like I am simply pressing against a wall. I shove them harder, and they slowly make way for me. I walk forward, still forcing them open until there is enough room to walk through.

The throne room is massive—like most places in this regal castle, except for my study.

The ceiling is probably forty feet high, and massive windows surround the room, filling it with daylight that reflects off the polished black, gray, and white tiled floor. Large pillars run along the enormous space and lead to the front of the room.

There, atop the wide stairs ahead, sits the Ruler on his lavish, red-cushioned throne. His elbow rests on the arm of the chair, and his chin rests on his fist. His black hair is pulled into a long braid trailing down his back, embodying the traditions of our tribal ancestors. He also wears long brown garments similar to those our ancestors would have worn.

Esteemed positions are held by certain kinds of people. The Commander and Seer positions, for instance, are represented by citizens who are of mixed descent, carrying the blood of both this land's natives and our tribal ancestors. It symbolizes the melded balance of key attributes from both sides, such as wisdom, brawn, peacefulness, and resilience.

The Ruler's position, however, is only held by direct descendants of the tribe. This was determined long ago, back when our ancestors first arrived, for the tribe's ability to weather the vile storms and dangerous creatures of the Frozen Tundra before discovering this quiet and peaceful land—hence why the Ruler maintains signature aspects of the tribe's traditions. The Ruler position requires a strong leader who can guide our people through any vicious circumstances.

I proceed through the vast space, approaching the Ruler, with Steven still clanking behind me. The Ruler doesn't budge at first. As I come close enough to see his tanned skin, his narrow eyes, and the age in his face that has come from the weight of his responsibilities rather than from the passing of years, he begins to move. He lifts his head from his fist and watches me attentively, preparing for whatever purpose he has summoned me here.

Once I am a couple of feet away from the stairs to his throne, I stop and kneel with one knee to the ground in respect, as is the custom. I hear Steven's armor shift as he brings a fist over his chest and kneels behind me.

"You wished to see me, sire?" I inquire.

"Yes," the Ruler says.

Rather than addressing me from his throne, as is also the custom, he rises. I look up in surprise and stand as well. Steven's armor clanks as he does the same.

The Ruler descends the steps. "I was hoping … that I would get a moment of your time." He reaches the foot of the steps and stands right in front of me. He shifts his gaze to Steven.

There's a slight pause before Steven says, "Sire." And his armor clanks as he exits.

The Ruler wants to be alone with me, but I can't imagine what could call for such a strange circumstance. Judging by the pause, neither can his right-hand soldier. The Ruler *always* has at least one guard present—even when there is no credible threat. It's custom. And there are no secrets in this community—least of all from someone as close to the Ruler as Steven.

The Ruler steadily watches Steven as he retreats, ensuring adequate distance between us. I wonder if the Ruler only wants Steven to back away so that he isn't within hearing range. But after a few moments, I hear the echoing boom of the massive doors closing behind me. We are utterly alone.

The Ruler finally looks back down at me. "Now, to take care of business." He holds a steady gaze on me, piquing my curiosity, until he breaks the silence. "Come."

He turns, his hands clasped behind his back, and walks around the stairs to a little space behind his throne. I follow his lead, finding it peculiar that he would take me back here. No one really pays attention to this space. It's away from the main throne room, and it's small. If anything, this area should be reserved for the Ruler—not a place that even the Commander should visit.

The throne hovers high above us. Behind it is a waist-high wooden table with something green on top of it and little figurines. I look closely as we approach. I see little tufts of green on brown things that stand up off the surface and little boxes in weird shapes surrounded by odd standing figures.

I continue to observe as the Ruler walks to the other side of the table. Standing beside it, I see that the green tufts on brown sticks are actually trees and that the boxes are buildings. The surrounding figures are people, wearing various clothes.

I notice a small portion of familiar towers on the left. It's a castle. A large gray wall extends from the tall fortress and surrounds the entire table, encompassing the buildings and the people within it.

Within the wall is a candy store with two candy canes crossing one another over the doorframe, and a store sign hangs above them that reads "Hubbard's Sweets." Beside it is the shoe-repair store, with a black shoe as its emblem. Next to that is the bakery. Across the road is a tavern. I recognize all these buildings. But why are they modeled here? And what does this have to do with me?

"This," says the Ruler, "is Taliver."

Chapter 5

"This is Taliver," I state, more to myself than to the Ruler.

The Ruler nods.

"Why?"

"That"—the Ruler points at me playfully—"is exactly why I've called you here. Daia, I have a proposition for you."

He casually uses my name rather than addressing me by my title. We are relatively familiar with one another by now. He's met with me from time to time, discussing my progress and preparation for my position. He and the Seer have worked hand in hand, preparing me for my role and teaching me everything I know. But my relationship with the Ruler is not the same as my relationship with the Seer. Perhaps he feels we are familiar enough to become more casual.

I consider the relationship between the last Commander and the Ruler. To assist the Ruler with matters of governance, that Commander had to have a strong relationship with the Ruler—one of great mutual respect. *I* want to be that kind of leader and hopefully achieve the level of greatness that those before me did. Perhaps this is the beginning of that.

"I would like you to oversee the citizens," the Ruler says.

I look up at him in surprise.

"Just for a day," he adds. "I want to see how you handle yourself. Prove to me that you know the people and what you're doing. Show it to the citizens of Taliver. You will handle the Ruler's duties for the day."

My eyes trail down to the replica of the community between us. He wants me to take over his position for an entire day. This is unheard of. No one just assumes the position of the Ruler—not even for a day. Furthermore, only the heir of the Ruler or another direct descendant of our tribal ancestors can ever take over the rule of the community. I, however, am neither. The Ruler currently has no heir, and I am of mixed descent.

This seems to be some sort of test. But this is not related to the training of a rising Commander. Plus, I have already completed my training. I have my induction ceremony in only a couple of days. This task should be seen as an honor—an impossible, truly special honor. But something doesn't feel right.

"You're familiar with the community and the people," the Ruler says. "You know them well. Why don't you go out and tend to them first thing in the morning? Take note of their wants and needs. Then you can return and handle other responsibilities of the Ruler."

"You ... want me to rule these people?"

"Only for a day," he repeats. "You can do this. I know you can. I've seen how well you've trained and how seriously you take your responsibilities. You know the ins and outs of this community."

His sudden confidence in me causes suspicion. He has just claimed that he wants me to prove myself and my capabilities to him. But now he is perfectly certain that I am capable and that I know exactly how to handle the community.

Seeming to catch himself, the Ruler grins widely. "I'll see you tomorrow evening. You will take up the position first thing in the morning. Steven will be assigned to assist you. He is familiar with the Ruler's responsibilities, and I will give him instructions on how to aid you. You may stay here for a moment and further acquaint yourself with the model if it will be beneficial to you. Everything you need is right here."

He makes his way back to the front of the throne room.

Just as I begin to wonder what I am to do about my final session with the Seer tomorrow, the Ruler turns back to me with a finger up.

"And also … don't tell the Seer," he says quietly.

Without even giving me a chance to question this or to respond, the Ruler turns and disappears around the towering stairs.

I wait a few moments to see if he ascends on the other side of the stairs to sit on his throne above. It would be odd for him to leave me here alone, but he doesn't appear on the steps. A moment later, I hear the massive doors open and then shut with a faint echo as the sound reverberates dully off the bright walls.

I turn back to the model of the community. He actually left me here alone. And why would he want an official task to be hidden from the Seer? Unless there *is* something suspicious and unsanctioned about his assignment.

Don't tell the Seer.

I've never kept anything from the Seer before.

Chapter 6

The Seer and I sit at an ornate dining table of polished, dark wood that is too long for just two people. We're in a large dining room near our quarters within the castle. The kitchen staff has made us boar meat and green vegetables, which we eat in silence.

A massive chandelier hangs too high above to even notice often, and a fireplace stands a few feet behind the Seer. I sit at the end of the table.

"So, how did your meeting with the Ruler go?" the Seer asks.

I search for the words to respond, mindful of the last instruction that the Ruler gave me. While the situation doesn't sit right with me, I don't want to defy orders. I have a place and a duty in this community, and the last thing I want is to violate that. For all I know, there could be a legitimate reason for it, which I just don't know about yet.

"It was ... eventful," I tell him.

"Eventful, you say?" says the Seer. "What did he want with you?"

"Oh, nothing special." I move some vegetables around on my plate. "He just wanted to discuss plans for the induction ceremony."

At this, the Seer drops his fork onto his plate and stares at me.

Noticing his gaze drilling into me, I look up at him, feeling a pang of guilt for lying to him and fearing that he somehow knows. I feign an innocent glance away before looking back at him. "What?"

"You're lying to me, Daia."

I know there's no sense in combating it. The Seer may be quirky, and he may not be the most put-together individual, but he knows me well. And when he draws a strong conclusion about something, that's it. There's no convincing him otherwise.

I drop my fork onto my plate with a loud clank that echoes off the walls and practically curdles my blood, but I don't care. I slump back in my chair, feeling hopelessly trapped between duty to my role and honesty with the Seer—a dilemma that should never exist in the first place.

"What happened?" he asks.

My eyes wander down to my plate, contemplating how to answer. Why am I defending the Ruler? I guess it's because he's the Ruler, known for being "always faithful, always true." He's a caring, protective leader, not a corrupt one. And he helped teach me everything I know. But still, I can't shake this feeling that something is wrong.

I take in a deep breath and huff it back out. "All right." I sit back up at the table. "The Ruler put me in charge of his duties. I have to … prove myself and my capabilities to him."

The Seer's face suddenly changes into a deep, disapproving frown. "The Ruler wants to test you by giving away his position … to you?"

"But only for one day."

"And why didn't you tell me this?" he asks.

I shake my head, feeling silly for the reason I'm about to give after seeing the Seer's reaction, which clearly confirms my suspicions. The truth is, though, there's no other reason to give. "Because he told me not to. And I wasn't sure why."

The Seer just stares at me, his frown managing to burn a hole into my soul.

"What?" I ask, though I'm sure I already know his answer. I don't know what else to say, though.

The Seer takes a moment before answering, almost seeming disappointed in me for not acting on this sooner. "You know exactly what. He told you to hide something from me—a training assignment … from your trainer. There are no secrets from your Seer. You know better than that. That's a violation of Taliver protocol."

Chapter 7

The Seer suggests that I follow the Ruler to see what he's up to. I think this is a bad idea, but the Seer is better at determining what actions need to be taken than I am. We finish eating, and he tells me he'll meet me in the study once he finds out what he can about where the Ruler will be tonight.

I don't believe that he'll be able to find anything out, but to my surprise, he does. I shouldn't be too surprised, though. The Seer has greater access to the Ruler's affairs than I do. I imagine the Seer sneaking into the Ruler's study and rummaging through important papers on a desk, searching for hints of the Ruler's whereabouts. I've never seen the Ruler's quarters or study. I've only met with him in the throne room.

"The Ruler should be in the kitchen," the Seer says. "Follow him there and see what he's up to."

I agree to do so, doubtful that the Ruler will still be there by the time I reach the kitchen. Still, I go.

A couple of hallways and numerous grand portraits later, I reach the kitchen by the dining room I was just in. I peek into the doorway, and to my surprise, there is the Ruler, oddly cloaked in an excessively traditional regal fashion. He wears his regal red cape and a golden crown, and he holds his tall golden scepter in hand. He speaks with a staff member dressed in a brown apron and a tall white hat with a wide, flat top.

Other culinary staff busily go about the ovens and massive shelves of inventory, cleaning up and putting things away after serving everyone dinner. I am careful to remain just outside the doorway to avoid being seen.

The Ruler and the staff member seem slightly agitated. The staff member speaks with his hands, and the Ruler looks rigid. I wonder if this could have something to do with the Ruler's peculiarity lately.

Once they finish speaking, the staff member swiftly walks away. The Ruler stands there for a moment. My mind races as to what they could possibly have said.

I worry that the Ruler will turn around and leave through this doorway, inevitably discovering that I am following him. I am too far from the nearest corner behind me to make it there in time, I'm sure. This is a very long hallway. I look ahead at the nearest corner, which is just a few yards from me, but I would have to cross the doorway and risk being seen.

With either option, I wouldn't be able to disappear before the Ruler spotted me. I could easily say that I was coming here to check on the kitchen staff in preparation for my assignment tomorrow, but I'd rather not have to try to make that evident lie believable.

After a moment, the Ruler finally straightens up with his scepter and, thankfully, marches forward through the kitchen, away from me. I recall there is another exit at the far end of the kitchen, which leads to a back corner of the massive dining room that the Seer and I ate in. Presumably, that's where the Ruler is heading.

Most of the kitchen staff wander through the inner doorway at the right side of the kitchen, toward the back. It's the designated section for handling dirty dishes and storing most of the food in large pantries that line the back wall. The section isn't completely sealed off from the front of the kitchen, though. It has a couple of large, glassless windows that open the section up to the main part of the kitchen, making staff members visible as they wash dishes just on the other side of the wall.

As the kitchen is pretty much empty, I peek in to look toward the exit on the far right and see the Ruler going to the dining room. He turns to walk diagonally farther into it, seemingly not intending to make a return trip through the kitchen.

I glance back at the staff behind the open wall and see everyone busily tending to their duties. The few staff members still on this side of the kitchen wall face away from me, taking care of the dishes and leftover food. Everyone's too busy to pay any attention to me, which is good. I don't want anyone to even consider that I am doing anything suspicious and alert the Ruler.

I sneak into the kitchen, tiptoeing and keeping my head down as I skitter along the tall shelves filled with ingredients and food products lining the center of the space. No one spots me as I reach the other doorway. I peek into the grand dining room and thankfully see the Ruler steadily approaching the main double doors, which lead into another hallway. I slip out of the kitchen before the staff notices me.

The Ruler steps into the hallway, but he doesn't turn right, into the one we both likely came from. He continues down the hall to the left, which surprises me. There are only two things down that path: the armory and the exit. At this late hour, I see no reason why he would be going to either.

There is no one else in the dining room, thankfully, so I freely rush through it after him. I step out and watch him approach the intersection at the end of the hallway. To the left is the armory. To the right is the exit. Of the two, I expect him to go right. To my surprise, though, he goes left.

I am about to rush to the corner and see what he is doing when I recall that the intersection ahead is really the only exit from the armory. There is a secret staircase descending to the dungeon from within the armory, but it is highly unlikely that the Ruler is going there. Then again, this whole scenario is highly unlikely.

Forced by instincts instilled in me by training, I prepare for the worst-case scenario of his return. I backtrack to the nearest corner behind me and check the other hallway. No one is there, so I step around the corner and peek out from behind it, waiting to observe the Ruler's return. Thankfully, at night, these halls are empty.

Sure enough, a few moments later, here comes the Ruler. However, he doesn't come back down this hallway to turn in for the night. Rather, he continues straight to the other side of the intersection, which leads to the exit.

I quickly scurry back into the hallway and rush to the intersection up ahead. I peek around the corner and watch as the Ruler approaches the large, ornate wooden doors. He pushes them open and steps into the cool evening with a morning star weapon in hand.

Chapter 8

I go after the Ruler, knowing that I probably shouldn't. I crack one of the massive doors open just to peek through. The moon dimly reflects off Taliver, as replicated by that model in the throne room. On the main road, which features most of the community's shops, the Ruler is speaking with someone near the bakery. I cannot really make out the man in the darkness of the night, though. They shortly end their conversation, and the Ruler starts to walk farther along the road.

I watch as he passes every building along the way without sparing them a single glance. Then I realize where he's going. He's approaching the large black gate at the end of the road, which marks the way out of the community and beyond the wall of defense.

I stare after him in surprise for a moment, wondering what business he could possibly have outside Taliver. I'm not sure if *he* is up to something suspicious, or if he's protecting the community from something suspicious. Either way, something is clearly wrong, and he's keeping me out of it, which makes me concerned for the community that I am supposed to protect.

I go to covertly slip out of the castle when a firm hand grabs my arm from behind and yanks me back inside.

"What are you doing?" the Seer demands in a loud whisper, with flaming eyes.

"I'm following the Ruler," I whisper back, pushing his hand off my arm. It was starting to dig into my skin in a very unpleasant manner.

"You can't go outside," the Seer says.

I look at him. "Why not? This was your idea."

"That was before he went outside in the dead of night. Where is he going?"

"It looks like he's leaving Taliver."

The Seer squeezes his lips together and sighs. "You need to stay here."

He takes my arm again and turns to drag me through the hallways of the castle. I pull myself up short and shove his hand off again.

"I'm not going back," I tell him. "I'm following the Ruler."

Earlier I was not entirely thrilled about this little mission, but now I feel determined. I don't know why the Ruler is keeping me out of whatever is going on, but I have a duty to fulfill to my community as the Commander—to my citizens—even if I haven't officially taken on my role yet.

I turn around, and, to my surprise, the Seer tries to grab me again. However, the instant that his hand makes contact with my skin, I yank my arm out of his reach. I look at him in astonishment. He has never been so forceful before.

"What is going on?" I demand. "Why won't you let me follow him? This was your idea."

"You don't know the lands out there. They are freezing, dangerous, and packed with storms."

Clearly, he will say anything to get me to abandon my pursuit. We don't get storms in these lands. I would have to travel farther beyond the defensive wall to reach that kind of dangerous territory, like the Frozen Tundra, which the Seer was talking about earlier.

Then I realize he believes that the Ruler is going out to the Frozen Tundra.

"He's not staying nearby, is he?" I ask.

The Seer holds my gaze for a moment and then shakes his head. "It's not likely, no. The Ruler doesn't just leave the community. And if he does, it is probably for a very significant reason—one that requires more than stepping just outside Taliver's wall. It requires a journey of greater distance."

I nod, knowing that the Seer won't let this go. He is much too concerned for my safety in the event that the Ruler really does go out to the Tundra—not to mention what circumstances I might be getting myself involved with or what consequences I could face if the Ruler catches me. The Ruler is not known for being cruel, but he doesn't accept defiance either. The Seer tends to be protective of me, but he also needs to understand that this is my responsibility. This is the very thing he's trained me for.

"All right," I falsely concede.

He nods and turns to walk me down the hallway back to my quarters. As soon as he turns his back, though, I feel a pang of guilt in my chest as I swiftly pivot around and dart through the door.

The Seer turns, but it's too late. I'm already out of his reach.

Chapter 9

The Ruler is walking through the black gate. I scurry down the wide stairs of the castle and chase after him in the shadows. I am too far out for the Seer to come after me. He's not the running type.

The guilt lingers. I've never defied the Seer before. He's always been my confidant and the mentor who's molded me into the person I am today. I don't want to be at odds with him, but this is important. This is a matter of my people's safety. This is my responsibility.

I run along the path through the marketplace until I get close to the gate. I step off to the right of the path and squat beside the wall, peering around it to see the Ruler descending the stairs as the gate slowly closes. I'm careful to stay out of sight—not so much for fear of whatever punishment would ensue if I were caught but because I know I will never get another opportunity to find out what is really going on. I'm grateful for my training, particularly from the Seer, which has taught me how to be stealthy and clever when needed.

Taliver stands on top of a hill that overlooks a valley. On the way down, a waterfall spews out of the hill and flows into a river below. I've rarely set foot outside Taliver—only to study the surrounding safe lands before reaching the Tundra. From those rare occasions, I remember that you have to be careful walking near the waterfall. The loose ground could give way and send you sliding down to your impending doom. The Seer and I almost slipped a couple of times.

The Ruler doesn't walk straight down near the waterfall, though. He turns around, facing me, to walk past the stairs and alongside the wall. I wait before moving because I can see his eyes from here, which tells me that he could see me if I drew attention to myself.

Once he's beyond view, I surreptitiously squeeze through the gate before it fully closes and climb down the steps, careful that I am never in sight of the Ruler. Staying to the left side of the stairs—as far away from the Ruler as possible—I don't see even the tip of his head, which is good for now.

I reach the bottom and peek around the stairs. It takes me a while to find him in the dark, but I eventually spot his silhouette descending the far slope.

He must not have wanted to descend the hill directly in front of the gate to ensure no one could spot him from within Taliver. Beside the wall, he's hidden from anyone inside the community.

Since I'm within his peripheral vision, I wait for him to get farther down the hill before I follow. Once I do, I realize that there's no path here. So, I carefully take each step alongside the wall, bracing my hands against it for stability and hoping with all my might that I don't slip or kick a rock down the hill, alerting the Ruler to my presence. I stop where the Ruler did and descend behind him.

He reaches the foot of the hill and walks into the open valley, which is filled with a few clusters of trees, the river, and grass—lots of grass. Even in the darkness, I can see the beautiful green pastures extending as far as the eye can see, illuminated by the bright half-moon in the starry sky. But I know that the beauty only extends so far. Just beyond the horizon is the Frozen Tundra.

I dodge protruding rocks and potentially noisy branches and leaves as I descend the slope after the Ruler. As I do, I wonder if he has ever snuck out like this before. How many times has he vanished without anyone noticing? Perhaps his little discussion with the kitchen staff was solely to create an alibi to eliminate any possible suspicion of his absence from the castle. Perhaps it was simply to make things appear normal— even though, clearly, they're not.

I manage to reach the bottom of the hill without attracting attention to myself. I continue to walk behind the Ruler across the valley, surprised as I realize that he has not yet checked over his shoulder to make sure no one is following him. Not even once. He keeps walking across the valley, looking straight ahead, seemingly very confident in his clandestine endeavors.

He veers broadly right toward a mass of trees a few yards ahead. I follow, wondering what plans he has in there. The collection of trees is bordered by another hill, which is rocky, and I wonder if he intends to climb it. That would be difficult, considering he's mysteriously carrying his scepter.

After a while, he enters the grove, and I lose him in the shadows. I become extremely uneasy because I cannot see him while I am clearly out in the open. I swiftly move under the cover of the trees, worried that he might have already spotted me, and look around.

In the open plain outside these trees, the loudest thing was the glow from the moon in the sky. Here, the soft sound of the rustling trees is a huge contrast to the still silence of the night. I watch the leaves in the trees sway like they're dancing in the wind. I would expect some small, harmless creatures to be visible in the branches, but they must all be asleep. I only see the trees and the shadows.

My attention is snapped back to what I am doing out here when I sense something shift around me. I listen attentively, wondering if I will hear voices from a secret meeting involving the Ruler, but I hear nothing.

Something shifts in my peripheral vision to my right, and there—there he is. The Ruler stands there with his scepter, but my heart leaps into my throat because I can't tell if he's facing toward me or away from me. I hope with everything inside me that he hasn't spotted me yet.

The shadow walks forward, and my heart jumps even higher into my throat as he approaches.

He's found me!

Chapter 10

I open my mouth, searching for words, but I can't find any.

The Ruler's silhouette gets closer, and I feel more pressured to say something.

"Sire" is all that I manage.

He comes right in front of me with his scepter in hand. "You followed me."

"No. I ..." I worry about the consequences. A sentence to the dungeon? Loss of my title? And then who would discover what's really going on with the Ruler? Repercussions for the Seer? Then I remember what happened to the last Seer, and I worry even more.

The Ruler comes to a halt in front of me. "No. You followed me," he repeats.

I open my mouth to respond, still not knowing what to say, but the Ruler interrupts.

"Just as I knew you would."

I look at him in confusion. "Huh?"

"You are not like other officials in training, Daia. You have a curious spirit and a determined heart. I knew you'd follow me. And at the very least, even if you didn't, the Seer is a very curious man himself. He would have surely sent you."

That would explain why he didn't check to see if he was being followed. He intentionally set me up, using himself as bait. But why?

"So, which is it?" he asks. "Did you come out here on your own, or did the Seer send you?"

"Why did you lure me out here?" I ask, ignoring his question. I glance down, recalling the journey I just went on, following him through the castle. I spot his free hand—the one not clinging to the scepter—and see that the weapon is missing. "And why would you take the morning star?"

Normally, a subject shouldn't question the Ruler. It's a sign of disrespect and forgetting one's place. However, these are exceptional circumstances, and he lured me into following him here for something. I have the right to ask questions, and I'm sure he knows it.

"Ah," the Ruler says. "The morning star. Yes. Yes." He returns to where I first spotted him a few yards away. He bends down to retrieve something lying on the ground behind a tree. As he walks back to me, the morning star swings in his hand. "This was a prop to keep your attention. I wanted to talk to you out here about the Seer."

Alarm triggers a prickling at the back of my mind as I again remember what happened to the last Seer.

"He's … a little confused on things," the Ruler says.

I continue to stare at him as blankly as possible, not giving any thoughts or suspicions away in my expression.

"No doubt he told you about what happened with the Seer before him."

I don't want to respond, feeling it may violate the trust the Seer has placed in me.

The Ruler nods. "I suspected as much. And of course, my request for confidentiality was trumped by your relationship with the Seer, wasn't it? You told him that I was putting you in a leadership role over the citizens for a day, though I told you not to."

I look away. While the Ruler knows that my relationship with the Seer far outweighs my relationship with him, the truth is I defied his orders. I say nothing, but that is all the confirmation that the Ruler needs.

"Good," he says, almost sounding cheery. "Then you will want the best for him."

My attention shifts back to the Ruler.

"He is a threat, Daia, believing and claiming his Seer to have been murdered by officials of Taliver. He is bound to go around and tell others at some point. He has to be exiled, Daia—unless the truth can be revealed to him."

I stare at the Ruler in shock. How could he even consider such a thing? "Exile? No. You can't exile the Seer."

"I don't want to, but look at the options, Daia. Either I can risk that he spreads his beliefs throughout the entire community and causes conflict within Taliver, or I can remove him so that he is no longer a problem."

Despite how much I don't like the Ruler's words, I already know no protest from me will amount to anything. I can see his logic in preserving Taliver's peace, but exiling the Seer?

It sounds barbaric. It sounds … just like what happened to the previous Seer.

"He wasn't actually murdered by any officials in Taliver, Daia," the Ruler says. "I know what he told you. I've had this conversation with him many times before, but he won't believe me. The previous Seer had a son, who he didn't get along with. His son found him out there. There was a squabble, and he murdered his father. The son was also exiled immediately after the event."

"The current Seer doesn't know about the son?"

"The current Seer chooses to believe what he wants to."

I don't understand why the Seer would blatantly disregard the Ruler's explanation. However, honestly, I'm not so sure the Ruler is telling the truth after all the deceit and suspicious activity I've seen already.

I suddenly recall the Ruler's earlier conclusion that I care about the Seer's well-being. Clearly, he is going to propose an alternative option to exile.

"Well, then what am I supposed to do?" I ask.

The Ruler looks at me for a moment. "You have to find the son and convince him to come back so that he can explain everything to the Seer himself."

Perhaps this really will remove the threat that the Ruler feels from the Seer. Perhaps it won't. I can't tell if the Ruler is telling the truth or not, but if there is a chance that the Seer will be exiled, I have to do whatever I can to prevent that from happening. And I have to verify the truth for myself, because as this night progresses, I'm growing increasingly concerned about the Ruler's integrity and reliability in his reign. If he's not the "always faithful, always true" Ruler that we've been led to believe he is, then what kind of Ruler holds our citizens' lives in the balance?

I recall where the Seer told me his exiled predecessor lived. I look at the Ruler, realizing what this means. It seems the Seer had a reason to be concerned about my well-being tonight after all.

"In the Frozen Tundra," I conclude.

The Ruler nods slowly.

Chapter 11

And so here I am, freezing cold in a cave in the middle of the Frozen Tundra, shivering, and all because the Ruler sent me on a covert mission. He stands there, pretending to be furious with me for "sneaking" out of Taliver. Of course, he can't say that he sent me out here. That would cause a slew of questions and suspicions from Petrus and other citizens in Taliver about what is clearly a sensitive matter.

I still don't understand why the previous Seer would be exiled or why his son would kill him. Nor do I understand why I've never heard anything about these major events before, but I will discover the truth behind it all soon enough, when I find this son the Ruler has been talking about.

Meanwhile, I have to take the blame and follow the Ruler's lead, pretending that I defied orders. It bothers me that he so easily sacrifices my credibility for the cover-up and that he even put me in this position by bringing Petrus out here, but it's a good thing he did. Otherwise, I might not be alive right now, huddled and recovering in these extra blankets. I didn't know just how brutal it is out here.

Petrus looks concerned and tries to stand up for me, sure that there has to be a reason I would do something so rash. Poor Petrus has no idea just how futile his efforts are. The Ruler already knows all too well why I'm out here—and it isn't because I violated community guidelines. I refuse to tell Petrus anything, though I'm concerned about how this makes me look to the very soldiers I'm supposed to lead soon. I try not to think about that. Handling this situation is the priority right now.

Soon we are all gathered by the fire and drifting off to sleep. It's ironic that the Ruler, like Petrus, is directly descended from our tribal ancestors, which means that he has that thick, warm blood. Yet, I am the one who actually has to go out in this bitter cold.

While I still respect the Ruler for the position he holds, the truth is I've been set up. I was put in the middle of a squabble that does not involve me. What's worse, the Ruler lied to me. He lied about giving me the responsibilities of the Ruler for a day, knowing I'd follow him and he'd send me out here. He manipulated me, knowing I would tell the Seer what he asked me not to. Now I'm uncomfortable with how easily he both threatens to exile the Seer, a truly loyal official in the community, and frames me as a rebellious rogue.

As the sun begins to break through the night, I take the extra blankets I've been using to recover from the storm, get up while the other two are still sleeping, and tiptoe toward the mouth of the cave. Looking ahead, I discover the intensity of the blizzard has lessened. Earlier I could hardly see a couple of yards through the snowflakes, they were whipping around so violently. Now things are a bit clearer, enough to see a useful distance in front of me.

"Daia," I hear behind me.

I turn and find the Ruler following me. He comes to my side and walks with me toward the exit.

"The old Seer's son is over there." He points to the foot of a snowy mountain close enough that it can just barely be seen through the wind in the breaking dawn. It's maybe a mile away. "Remember to tell him that I sent you."

My eyebrows scrunch together as we stop just before the mouth of the cave. "You two seem on oddly familiar terms," I observe without desiring to look at him.

"I trained with him."

This catches me off guard. The rising Ruler doesn't train with anyone. There is only one Ruler, so they undergo instruction alone with the Seer—even when training in combat. Unless …

"He's my brother," he says.

My jaw practically drops. So, there *is* a possible heir. If that's the case, then this "son" that I'm about to find could succeed the Ruler. However, this would also make the prior Seer the Ruler's father.

"So, the late Seer," I start, "he was the Ruler before you."

The Ruler doesn't say anything. He just stares into the frigid storm outside.

"But he trained the current Seer—"

"The late Seer wasn't a Ruler," he concedes.

I look at him in surprise, trying to piece things together. This man isn't the true heir to the crown! The line of Rulers is an unbreakable chain of successors, and it's common knowledge that the prior Ruler did in fact have an heir. So how did the line break?

"There were suspicions that my father, the Seer at the time, would attempt to break the line of succession," the Ruler continues. "The prior Ruler had recently passed away—cause of death, unknown—and that was when my father wanted to infiltrate the system. He was discovered by an elite band of citizens who had been temporarily assembled in place of the late Ruler, since the heir—who, naturally, was under the Seer's care—was so young.

"My father's actions were considered treasonous, so they cast him out. Little did anyone know, the swap had already occurred, and my brother ..." He laughs in contempt. "My brother was the one taken into exile when it was supposed to be me. He's not my brother by blood, of course, though we were as close as brothers at the time. He was the true heir to the crown, not me. No one ever really saw the young heir back then, though. So, while the heir was under the care of my father in place of the late Ruler, it was very easy for the swap to take place right underneath everyone's noses.

"My father had already been preparing, training us together. The heir was too young to fully understand all that was going on, I'm sure. Or at least, I thought he was. Then he grew up and seemingly learned who he is. As for my father, I can assure you ... no one in Taliver killed him. It was my brother."

I stand frozen, but not from the cold. I try to digest everything, one fact at a time. It's a lot to take in: treason, infiltration of the system, the broken chain of pure tribal-descendant Rulers ... Presumably, the late Seer was of mixed heritage, which would mean that the Ruler is too.

I think about the Ruler's conclusion earlier that I would share information with the Seer. He didn't believe that I would keep information to myself. So, why share these dark secrets with me that could tear—no, that *would* tear— the community apart if revealed? I can't tell if I should believe his preposterous story or if he's trying to manipulate me again.

"Why are you telling me all of this now?" I ask.

The Ruler shrugs almost nonchalantly. "Well, if *I* don't tell you"—he turns and meets my gaze as he retreats into the cave—"I have a slight idea that someone else just might."

And he returns to the fire.

I look back at the snowy mountain across the terrifyingly cold terrain, focusing my eyes on the foot of the mountain: my destination. As I do, a new thought occurs to me that I was too distracted with worry for the Seer to realize before. The Ruler knows that the Seer has suspicions regarding the preceding Seer's death. But the Seer couldn't have shared those suspicions without divulging the fact that he'd violated orders and left Taliver to continue his training with an exile, which he specifically told me he has kept secret.

So how does the Ruler know that the Seer suspects anything about his predecessor's death or that the Seer snuck out for training? And how much have I unintentionally confirmed by not denying these accusations? How much trouble is the Seer really in right now? And how many secrets and lies are shrouding our community?

Chapter 12

The storm may be calmer, but it's still brutal. It's not the kind of storm that caresses your cheek with light snowflakes or nudges you with gentle winds. These storms are fierce. They're the brutal storms that our tribal ancestors endured.

Every flake is heavy, and it pummels my skin with an intense, icy burn. The wind is worse, shoving into me like a brick wall over and over again until it pauses. Then it picks back up again with a vengeance—several times from a different direction. I lean my weight hard against the wind, trying to plant each step so that I don't get carried away into another dangerous lake—all the while trying not to stumble in the inconsistent gusts.

I hold the thick blankets from the cave as my shield in the storm. I make sure to include my nose and mouth under their covering, thinking the colder the air that I breathe, the worse off I'll be. About halfway to the mountain, though, a sudden gust of wind catches me off guard, and I don't compensate with my grip on the blankets in time. They're suddenly ripped from my hands and carried away in the wind, leaving me exposed to the cold again.

I can't go back to the cave for another one and risk Petrus being awake and the Ruler forcing me back into pretending to be a rebellious citizen. They'll take me back to Taliver to face whatever consequences await me, and I may never get another chance to sneak away to find out the truth. No. I'm too close to the answers I need. I've got to press on. I use my arms to guard my face against the battering flakes. The cold ... I try with all my might to ignore it creeping back into my bones.

Natives of Taliver could never withstand such frigid turmoil, but descendants of our tribal ancestors ... well, we've endured our share and developed hereditary adaptations to this. Otherwise, there would be no way I could survive this.

Already I'm just as bad as—if not worse than—I was when the Ruler and Petrus found me. My body shivers so violently that my breaths are unsteady, and I can't hold my arms still over my face. The warmth I absorbed from that cave fire could only last so long in this wretched climate. I feel my body wearing out with exhaustion, and I can only hope that I'll reach this person's residence soon.

Eventually, a little log cabin near the mountain comes into view through the fierce storm. I'm relieved at the sight of a golden glow that illuminates a little window on the side as smoke puffs out of the chimney poking from the slanted roof. *Warmth!* I try to pick up the pace, fighting the forceful wind with every step.

After finally reaching the cabin, I glance through the small, abnormally thick window and am reminded of what the Seer described when he peeked in through a window like this one all those years ago. Who knows? Maybe it was the same cabin.

Thankfully, all I see is a wooden table with food sitting on it and a wooden chair. There are no signs of an eerie murder, and someone clearly lives here. The setting looks very similar to the description the Seer gave, though.

I make it to the door and struggle as I force my shaking arm up and give a single knock. I wait for someone to answer, too weak and exhausted to knock more than once. I just hope that someone heard it.

No one comes, though. Surely, they have to be here in the midst of this insufferable storm. I don't want to stay out here. I need warmth. I *need* it! I gather whatever strength I have left to force my arm up and ferociously rap on the door with all my might.

Rap, rap, rap, rap, rap, rap, rap—

"All right! All right already!" an agitated voice calls.

I stop knocking and fold my arms together, unable to stop the violent shakes plaguing my body from the ice that has seeped seemingly deeper into my bones than before.

I step back as heavy footsteps clomp to the door. Suddenly, more tangible whips of the wind smack into my back, and I thrust my arms out with strength I didn't know I still had to brace myself against the doorframe as the storm pummels me.

The door opens.

"Can I help you?" a man asks me.

"C-can I c-come inside?" I ask between chattering teeth, too tired to pay attention to his rude, standoffish posture. He seems to take note of my condition before he reluctantly backs away and opens the door wider.

I release the frame, giving in to the gusts, and practically fly into the warm cabin. I notice the hot fire in the far wall, with a mantel over the fireplace—the source of the chimney smoke I saw outside—as my bones immediately begin to thaw. It's so warm in here it feels like the sun, even though I know it's not that hot. The ruthless wind still howls and bangs against the cabin. I'm so grateful to be safe from its merciless lashes and the cold's relentless bite. Exhausted and still freezing, I find myself shivering and holding my arms while feeling like I might collapse.

I hear the man close the door behind me. There's a slight pause before his footsteps travel to my right somewhere. Before I know it, he's at my side with a small wooden chair. He wraps a blanket around me, and I cling to it for dear life as he takes me by the shoulders and sits me down in the chair.

Without a word, he disappears while I close my eyes, soaking in the warmth. I open my eyes as his footsteps quickly return, and I find a steaming brown mug with a leaf design in front of my face. He must have just been making a warm beverage as I arrived, which is fortunate for me. It smells minty and strong, but I don't question it.

I take the cup and feel the heat against my freezing hands. Truthfully, they're not ready for this kind of direct heat yet. The warmth almost feels like it burns my hands, but I don't care. I'm grateful for it. As I enjoy the heat from the cup, blowing on it so I can drink, the man walks past me and then comes back with a chair, which he sets down to face me.

He sits there silently as I take small sips from the mug. The concoction tastes minty and gives my mouth a tingling sensation as the heat slithers from the tip of my tongue down into my stomach. After a while, I'm still cold, but I'm already feeling so much better.

Feeling more like myself again, I begin to take proper notice of my surroundings, like I'm waking from a slumber. I see a little kitchen area through a small walkway behind the man.

The mantel over the fireplace holds small, folded pieces of paper—cards. In front of the fireplace is a small couch and a coffee table. A small, round, wooden table stands off to the side of the room, behind me, by the window that I looked through. That must be where the chairs we're sitting on belong.

I look at the man. He's about the Ruler's age, with tanned skin and short, messy dark hair. He wears a white robe and green slippers over tall green socks. Oddly enough, he reminds me of the Seer.

He shrugs. "All right. What are you doing in my house?"

Clearly, he doesn't like to have visitors.

I take another drink from the mug. "I'm here under strict orders," I answer, intentionally remaining vague. It feels rude, especially after he's shown such hospitality to a total stranger, but I want to see what I can get out of him before I give anything away.

The man widens his eyes in fake astonishment. "Oh, well, please, Your Majesty." He bows dramatically in his chair.

He's not going to give me anything. I can tell. He's much too cold and sarcastic, likely from a lifetime of being out here all alone. Even if he did give me something, I'm not sure I could trust him to be honest. I need to test him for the truth—push him and see if I can get some kind of genuine reaction out of him.

"That's ironic, considering your birthright."

The man looks up from his little seated bow in surprise and straightens. "Why are you here? Who sent you?" Judging by his reaction, that part is true. He really *is* the true heir to the crown. But there are still many claims that need to be confirmed.

"Your brother did," I answer.

His expression drops to a blank look, as though he's just seen a ghost. I don't know if his reaction is due to the mere mention of his brother or the fact that his brother is the reason I'm here, but I know how to get down to the truth. My training has taught me the value of strategy. So, I decide to test an angle that I'm sure he'll be interested in, if everything the Ruler told me is true.

"How would you like to get your throne back?" I say.

Chapter 13

"My brother? You came here because of my brother?" the man asks me.

"Yes," I say. "Is that so hard to believe?"

He looks down in thought before returning his attention to me. "Did he tell you about me?"

"Not much," I lie. "Just that you trained together and that you could have become the Ruler."

The man groans, squeezing his lips together and looking away. Then he gets up and walks toward me. "Get out."

This takes me by surprise. "Wh-what?"

He already has his hands against my back and is shoving me up and to the door so quickly I drop the blanket and the mug.

"I said, get out!"

He grabs the doorknob and turns it, but I twist out of his grasp before he can pull the door open.

"What do you mean, get out? Don't you want to get back what's rightfully yours?"

He points at me. "You just said he only stated that I could have been the Ruler. Now you say that the role is rightfully mine. What did he really tell you?"

"Nothing," I claim, though I know he is already aware that I know more of the story than I'm letting on. I quickly try to distract him from his suspicions. "But surely your place is in Taliver rather than out here."

He pauses as though considering whether to say something. But then he gives a curt shake of his head, and he grabs my arm while he reaches for the doorknob again.

I spin out of his hold another time, frustrated that he keeps trying to haul me back outside into the bitter storm. "What is wrong with you?"

"I don't want to have this conversation, all right?"

"Why not?" I dodge another of his attempts to grab me.

"Because I just don't!" He reaches again and misses.

I wonder what's holding him back from his responsibilities in Taliver and making him so excessively defensive if he's really the rightful heir. He should be leaping for the crown. Why is he refusing it? What is he not telling me?

"Why are you avoiding this?" I ask.

"Because I don't want to talk about it."

"But why?"

"Because I don't *want* to!"

"Why not, though?" I ask, seeing an opportunity as he is clearly beginning to break. "You're the rightful heir to the throne of Taliver. The crown was taken away from you. And you don't even care to take it back? Why not? What has you so determined to refuse the very thing you're meant to—"

"Because I'm scared!" he bursts out.

This pulls me up short. I was definitely not expecting that answer.

"I can't go up against my brother. Not again."

So, the Ruler *didn't* tell me everything after all. By the looks of it, this man wasn't just "swapped" out of his role as heir to the crown. There was something more. There was something more that *broke* him, and I've just struck a nerve that's still wounded by it. My confident, demanding demeanor is replaced with sympathy, and I start to really wonder what exactly happened between the two of them.

The man abandons me to circle around his couch and plop down in front of the fire.

I sit on the other side of the couch, looking for the right, sensitive way to get him to keep talking. I open my mouth, but I don't know this man well enough to know what will console him while encouraging him to say what's on his mind. He gets the hint, though.

"I have challenged him before. We had to compete with each other for the crown. It was a series of tests: strategy, combat … several things. We grew up around each other, as close as brothers, but he never did anything fairly. He beat me up considerably when I was younger. He was older than me and grew bigger before I did. He capitalized on that. He didn't even treat his own father properly." He shakes his head.

"Where was the Ruler at that time?" I ask. "And who conducted this challenge?"

"Julius did," the man says. "My father had already passed at the time, and as the Seer,

Julius's father had closer interactions with me than anyone else. After he had already swapped us and taken me under his care, I knew I could never claim that I had been kidnapped. He knew it too. No one had ever really seen me because I was so young. I would just be seen as a rogue citizen trying to take the crown.

"Julius said that he'd relinquish the crown to me if I managed to beat him. I didn't, but I knew that even if I somehow did win, I would never get the crown back, and he would never let me forget that. Same way he never let his father forget who the Ruler was." He scoffs to himself.

This piques my interest, as I would have thought being exiled would mean being outside the Ruler's jurisdiction.

"But I thought your f—I mean, his father was cast out by an elite band of citizens in Taliver," I say. "He wouldn't be under his son's rule."

"Who do you think gave the order for his exile?"

I look at him, unable to find words.

"The elite citizens weren't there *in place* of the Ruler. They stood *alongside* the Ruler as support. Nothing could be decreed or decided without the Ruler's say-so."

He sees that I'm still speechless and scoffs to himself again, shaking his head at the fire.

"So … the Ruler's father managed to make him Ruler, and then the Ruler turned around and cast his own father out?"

"Therein lies the moral of the story: don't trust that man."

"But … why?" I ask.

"He was likely greedy and pompous, didn't want to keep any remnants of his old life around, reminding him that he's not the true Ruler. Besides, all the better to get rid of the rightful heir, who could pose a threat to his power. So, he took the gift his father stole for him and cast his own father out along with me. Either that, or he blamed his father for his mother's death. She died of an illness, but"—he shakes his head—"Julius always blamed his father, saying that she probably died of disappointment."

I can hardly believe what I'm hearing, but I guess I shouldn't be surprised. Lately the Ruler has been showing himself not to be the "always faithful, always true" leader we thought he was. My greatest concerns are confirmed by every sentence in this conversation: the Ruler is unfit to lead our citizens. And right now, they are all left alone with him in power in Taliver. We have to get back to reveal the truth, deliver justice, and rescue the citizens before something terrible happens.

What I still can't understand, though, is why the Ruler would send me out here only to discover this hidden truth and put his reign at risk.

"That's why I don't bother with that man," the rightful heir says. "He's wrong. He's evil. He's crude. And I don't have time to deal with a miscreant like him."

"Well, you have to come back now. He's ruling over your people—sitting in a position that belongs to you. You really want your citizens to be subject to someone like him?"

He shakes his head at the fire, frowning. "It's out of my hands."

I jump up, aghast at his nonchalance. "No! It *is* in your hands! It's always *been* in your hands!" I exclaim. How can he not see that this is his responsibility—his *duty*—both to himself *and* to his people?

"No. I am out here, and he's not going to come anywhere near me. I'm good."

"No, he'll just send someone to you," I mutter underneath my breath, mindful of why I came here.

"There are only so many people he can send."

"He has an entire community!" I exclaim incredulously.

"No, he doesn't. Not an entire community of direct descendants of the tribal ancestors."

"Wh-what does that have to do with anything?"

He looks at me as though I am stupid. "Because only direct descendants can really survive the storms out here."

My face falls. "Wait. What?"

"You didn't know?"

I slowly shake my head, flashing back to the impossibility of my trek out here. Now I understand why the Ruler sent me out here to discover the truth. He knew I would never survive to tell it—assuming I even made it this far. I find it hard to grasp that he would do something so drastic, though. Yes, he is manipulative and dishonest, but would he really take it *this* far?

"N-no. No. He sent me out here to get you and bring you back."

"To bring me back? Sweetheart." He chuckles. "He doesn't want me back. How do you think his father died? Why do you think he cast him out? It wasn't just an exile. It was a death sentence. Mixed descendants can't survive out here."

He killed his own father. My eyes widen, and my heart pounds in my chest as I realize … I'm trapped here.

The man sees my reaction. "You're not a direct descendant, are you?"

I shake my head, not really willing to look at him.

Barely able to speak and with my jaw shaking, I say, "I was supposed to bring you back so you could explain to someone in Taliver that you killed your father."

For the first time, the man looks genuinely concerned—or sorry—for me. "He sent a mixed descendant out into the Tundra to bring the man he displaced from the crown back to Taliver to falsely explain how the father he himself murdered was supposedly killed by the rightful heir …"

Now that I know the truth, it all sounds so obvious. But that's the problem. I *didn't* know the truth. And I didn't know I was nothing but a disposable casualty to the Ruler.

"He didn't send you to retrieve me. He sent you to get rid of you. He sent you out here to die."

Chapter 14

"Are you all right? You don't look so good." The stranger reaches up to me, wondering whether he should try to steady me, no doubt.

I feel almost woozy. The Ruler—he wants me dead. He doesn't care about me at all. And what would he say to the community if I died out here?

She was rebellious—snuck out in the middle of the night and then snuck out again after we rescued her. She couldn't handle the pressures of her position. She just snapped.

It disgusts me, and nothing that the Seer could say in my defense would make a difference. What could he say? Tell the citizens of Taliver that the Ruler was going to make me Ruler for a day? So, we were suspicious, and

I followed the Ruler, after which I mysteriously disappeared? No one would believe that. And even if they did, the Ruler's story of how he and Petrus found me and cared for me would easily render any attempts to raise suspicion moot. Petrus saw me—"rebellious" and all. He would be considered an eyewitness. That's probably the reason the Ruler brought him out here when "rescuing" me. That's why the Ruler did everything that was peculiar—he was setting up a plan to get away with my murder.

And I fell right into his trap.

I collapse onto the couch, feeling incredibly stupid and realizing just how trapped I am. "How could he do this to me?"

The man scoffs again. "Well, that's Julius for you." He throws something small into the fire, making embers jump and dance in the air.

"What do we do?"

"Oh, now it's 'we,' huh?" he scoffs. "Before, it was all about what *I* have got to do. Now, all of a sudden, it's 'we.'" He shakes his head as he reaches for the coffee table to sort some papers into a neat pile. He gets up with them and turns to lean toward me. "Good luck with that," he says, and he walks away from the couch.

I'm left here, watching the dancing flames as I hear the man clean up the mess I made behind the couch when I dropped the mug. I can't help but think about how I could either be trapped here forever or die out there in the cold. Either way, I would never see the Seer again, and he'd be left forever with the mystery of my disappearance. And our people would be left under the dangerous, abusive reign of the Ruler, who would do who-knows-what to them.

Then I realize—the Ruler banked on more than just the Tundra keeping me from successfully making the trip back. He was confident that even if I made it this far, there would be no way his brother would be willing to return to Taliver. The Ruler was sure he had nothing to worry about. Otherwise, he wouldn't have sent me out here. He's confident that neither one of us will ever be a threat again, which means that his guard is more relaxed now than ever. I've already made it out here. If I can manage to convince this man to return with me, and then survive the trip back, I will have won an advantage that the Ruler would never see coming.

I turn on the couch to face the man, who now stands in the dark kitchen. Through the narrow doorway are ugly teal floor tiles, old-looking beige counters, and brown cabinets.

"You have to come back with me," I tell him.

The man looks up at me, dropping his papers on the floor in shock. "Excuse me?"

"The Ruler didn't bank on me reaching you. And I'm sure he didn't bank on you letting me in even if I did. And on top of that, he sure didn't bank on you being willing to come back with me."

I think back on the man's unfriendliness when I first arrived. The Ruler knew his brother would be reserved and unwelcoming. It would have just further fed his confidence in sending me out here.

"No," he says, shaking his head.

I observe that he doesn't sound as offended by the idea of returning as he did a moment ago.

I get up from the couch and walk over to him, standing in the narrow kitchen doorway. "Come with me."

"No. I'm not coming with you. Why can't you understand that?"

"Look, I know you're scared, but you have to trust me on this, all right? I know the Ruler. He wouldn't—"

"You *know* the Ruler?" he snaps at me. "The man who I presume you did *not* imagine would send you out here to die? Because I would certainly hope you didn't come all the way out here knowing that."

I sigh in frustration. "He wouldn't have sent me here to discover the full truth unless he felt absolutely certain that I couldn't get back to Taliver with you to tell it. So, let's surprise him. He won't be expecting us, so we'll have the advantage." I extend a hand to him.

The man says nothing, which I take as a good sign.

"He took your birthright," I push.

He just turns his head farther away from me.

"That has to bother you."

"What bothers me … is that you won't leave this alone," he growls.

I stare at his fury in surprise, and he holds my gaze for a moment. Then he gathers his papers from the floor, charges past me through the doorway, and stomps over to the round wooden table.

I look at him, observing his refusal to return to Taliver. Then I realize his disdain for my presence here and decide to use that to my advantage.

I cross the little space to him at the table and hold my hands behind me so that I can look at him with an innocent expression.

"Do you want me to leave you alone?" I ask.

Not taking his eyes away from his papers, he throws a quick sarcastic expression my way.

"Well, the way I see it, you're stuck with me. I can't go out there alone. I would need someone to escort me safely to Taliver."

"Wrong. I could stick your behind back out there and let you freeze to death."

I squint at him, almost amused by his pretense. "Yeah, but you wouldn't do that."

He drops his hands with the papers against his legs in annoyance and looks at me with exasperation.

I simply smile. "Either you deal with me for the rest of your life, or you can help me get back to Taliver."

He stares at me for a moment, and I think that I've got him. Unfortunately, though, he lifts his papers and continues reading.

He keeps going back to those papers. I need him to focus on these undeniable facts so that he will see reason and return to Taliver. It seems the best way to do that is to remove the distraction. So, I decide that's exactly what I'm going to do.

I shrug. "All right." I come around the couch and find a cup of water sitting on the corner of the coffee table. I look back up at him, seeing he is still preoccupied with his papers.

I take the cup of water, raise it high over his couch cushions so that he can clearly see what I'm doing, and slowly tilt it until massive drops begin to pound the furniture. It takes him a second, but then he looks up. His eyes widen with horror.

"What are you doing?" he yells, dropping the papers and rushing to grab the cup from me.

I let him.

"Oh, nothing. I'm just stuck here, remember?"

I casually walk around the couch as he rests the cup back on the table. While he's distracted, I go in for the kill and grab the papers. Before he can even see that I have them—let alone register what I'm doing—I race around to the fire and hold the papers just over the flames.

"No! Don't!" he pleads, reaching for them from where he stands in horror.

"Then come with me."

"Don't! Please, don't—"

"Then come with me!"

I don't enjoy this any more than he does. I'm practically pleading with him, but he won't even acknowledge what I'm saying. He just collapses his face into his hands, almost sobbing.

Confounded by his reaction, I look at the papers and read the first one.

Son,

I am proud of you. One day, you will amount to all the good that I know you are capable of.

Your father

I gasp and quickly throw them down on the floor, away from the fire.

Chapter 15

He calms down and slowly grabs the papers off the floor by the coffee table.

"I am—"

He raises a hand to silence me.

"I'm really sorr—"

He firmly raises it again with an angry expression. Maybe I took things a little too far.

He sits on the couch, staring at the papers, and I come around the coffee table to sit near him. We remain silent for a while, and I'm riddled with guilt. I try to find something worth saying during this time in which he really doesn't want me to say anything.

"They're all that I have left of my father," he explains.

"I understand," I say quietly. I notice that he doesn't interrupt me anymore. "I'm so sorry. I didn't know."

He squeezes his lips together. "He was so excited for me to become the Ruler after him. He used to talk to me about my duty to the citizens and about giving them the guidance and the protection that they deserve. I wanted to be just like him—until he died. Then, of course, the Seer—Julius's father—took advantage of the situation during one of our training sessions." He sighs and shakes his head. "I was too young at the time to really understand what was going on at first. And by the time I realized ..." He shrugs.

I can find no words to respond.

"He was a nice man, though. He took care of me well. He just ... he had a terrible son. He did wrong by me, yeah, sure. But he was just a parent who wanted his son to be happy. He would have done anything for his son's love." He blinks and takes a deep breath like he is coming out of a trance. "He deserved a better son."

I nod.

"All right." He braces his hands on his knees and grunts as he gets up. "Let's go."

I look up at him in confusion.

"Well, you don't believe you'll be able to get back without me, do you? And I have responsibilities. Like I said, I have a duty to the citizens, and they should have the guidance and the protection that they deserve. Besides, you're right. They're my people, and no, I don't want their lives to rest in the hands of someone corrupt like Julius. This situation *is* in my hands, and it's about time I did something about it. So …" He extends a hand to help me up.

I smile, glad that—though in a very unintentional way—something's finally convinced him to return to Taliver and set things right. I take his hand and get up.

"I'm Daia," I say, realizing that we don't even know what to call one another.

He nods. "Marquis."

Chapter 16

According to Marquis, the storm has phases. Sometimes it intensifies, and sometimes it abates. Marquis says that the storm will soon get worse than it was when I arrived, and we don't want to get caught in that. So, he grabs some extra layers, and we leave immediately.

Somehow, going back seems to take even longer than the journey to Marquis's house. It's probably because coming into the Tundra, I didn't know what I was stepping into. Now I do. And being stuck in the freezing temperatures and violent weather of the Tundra again, I would do anything to be in a warm place that doesn't beat me down.

Marquis shields me. He's wrapped me in some thick blankets and put on excessive, large garments, which he holds around me, encasing me in his body heat as we trudge through the storm. Despite the long way back, he never falters in shielding and protecting me. The forceful whips from the wind primarily lash him, but he's a strong man, and he withstands them.

The heavy snowflakes still smack against my face like pebbles, but Marquis bears the brunt of them. And of course, the freezing temperature is countered by his body heat. His efforts feel like they hardly make a difference because the storm is still rough, but the mere fact that I'm not freezing and suffering like I was before tells me this is a considerable improvement.

The key is covering the mouth and nose. Apparently, there's something in the storm's air that is hazardous to people who aren't immune like our tribal ancestors were—something even more dangerous than the cold itself. It makes a greater difference the more time a person spends in the Tundra, and it contributed to the last Seer's death after he was exiled. I make sure to keep my mouth and nose covered with the blankets during our trek back to Taliver. Even if I were to have stayed in Marquis's house while in the Tundra, it would have ended in my imminent demise eventually. I *have* to return to Taliver.

We take one break in a cave along the way. It's not the same one that I was in with Petrus and the Ruler—Julius, I realize ... not the same cave that I was in with Petrus and Julius. He is not the true Ruler.

This cave is farther along in the journey back to Taliver, which is good. It means there's a shorter distance remaining to reach our destination.

"So, what's the plan for tomorrow?" I ask Marquis, looking at him from the opposite side of the fire we've built.

"We'll figure it out when it gets here," he responds, holding his hands near the fire for warmth.

"We shouldn't just barge in there without a plan."

He looks up at me pointedly. "This isn't a revolt. This is returning power to its rightful place. We're not looking for a mutiny."

"Not mutiny, order. Julius's guard will be down, but he still has soldiers, power, and loyal citizens who don't know the truth about him. We can't just barge in there unless we want to be immediately sentenced to imprisonment or worse."

It's odd to think this way about the Ruler—about Julius—but I'm learning not to underestimate him.

Marquis pauses, considering my words. "What do you propose, then?"

"Well, first and foremost, we need to tell the citizens. They deserve to know the truth. Tomorrow is supposed to be my induction ceremony as Commander of the Forces."

Marquis's expression changes.

"Julius has probably already announced that I'm gone or dead, so the ceremony will likely be canceled already. There aren't any other major events tomorrow that I'm aware of, so we'll have to find a way to gather the citizens and—"

"No."

I freeze, looking at him. "We have to announce—"

"No," he says sternly.

I open my mouth to speak, but he continues.

"We go to Julius first and confront him. This is *his* error, and he has to make it right. Julius has done enough damage and put too many lives at risk, including yours. The people deserve to know the truth, but they also deserve it directly from his mouth, not from an official and a stranger to

Taliver. Besides, they'd have no reason to believe us. I'm sure Julius has been careful to build a good reputation, safe from even the possibility of any suspicious concerns regarding his reign. They need to hear the truth directly from him."

I want to say that this is a bad idea, but truthfully, Marquis is not wrong. This *is* Julius's responsibility, and he *should* be held accountable. I'm just not sure how compliant he'll be. Marquis is absolutely right about the citizens, though. They will have a hard time believing that their "always faithful, always true" Ruler is in fact a corrupt murderer seeking to maximize his power at anyone's expense. I still struggle with it myself.

I close my mouth and give a curt nod. "We'll go in the morning, right before when my ceremony would have taken place. Nothing should have filled that time in his schedule on such short notice, so he should be in his throne room. We should be able to avoid the majority of the guards then, if not all of them. This garment you gave me has a hood. I'll wear it over my face as we enter the community to ensure no attention is brought to us. That way, we can get to Julius and confront him before he catches wind of our presence and has the chance to apprehend us."

Marquis nods in agreement. "You should get some sleep." He lies down to get some rest himself. "Head Daia," he adds.

I smile across the fire at his acknowledgment of my title, and I lie down as well. I wonder if I should keep what I want to say to myself. I decide one quick little statement shouldn't hurt.

"I'm sorry for what Julius did to you," I tell him.

Marquis opens his eyes in the dancing glow of the fire as it flickers across his face. "I'm sorry for what he did to you."

I raise my eyebrows. *Good point*, I think to myself, and we both drift off to sleep.

Chapter 17

We rise early the next day and arrive at Taliver soon after. Leaving the Tundra and entering the valley just outside Taliver is such a relief. I'm so grateful to see greenery and warm bodies of water again. It's beautiful to see the blue sky and the fortified castle sitting up ahead on the hill with the waterfall, surrounded by flying birds and a nice, warm temperature. My skin tingles all over as it thaws.

As we near the community's gate, I pull my hood over my face. The gatekeeper meets us and requires us to state our business. He looks young and has short brown hair. I realize there was no gatekeeper the night I left. Perhaps that's what I saw that night, when Julius was speaking with someone on the main street of Taliver. Perhaps he was getting rid of the gatekeeper. I don't know.

I accede and step forward to state who I am, but the gatekeeper immediately recognizes me under the hood and lets us in. The gatekeeper is not utterly astounded to see me alive, which tells me that Julius has not yet announced my death or disappearance. I can't imagine why. This also tells me that the induction ceremony must still be expected to take place today. I look back at Marquis, who just glances at me without giving any surprise away.

I half expect Marquis to look around in wonderment as we enter through the gate, having not seen Taliver for so long, but he doesn't. I didn't realize it before because I was so grateful to have made it back to survivable terrain, but he didn't even admire the beautiful valley as we stepped out of the Tundra. He just continues to look straight ahead, dead on and probably deep in thought. I don't disturb him.

We walk through the busy streets, which are far more active than when I came through them a couple of nights ago. People hustle and bustle back and forth across the road to different stores and stands in the marketplace. There's a stand with some kind of green fruit to my left. On my right are some colorful pastries. Ahead I see the main bakery and all the other buildings I know of and saw in that model of Taliver that Julius showed me the other day.

We reach the castle and ascend the stairs, entering as inconspicuously as possible. I take Marquis through the halls to the throne room—Marquis's throne room. As we near the doors, I take my hood off. Steven stands guard. Upon seeing us, he looks confused and begins to inquire as to whether he can help us. I ignore him, because he can't help us. Only one person can.

I walk straight up to the doors and shove them open without waiting for Steven to escort us inside. A subject never approaches the Ruler unannounced, but as far as I'm concerned, this is not the Ruler. Marquis is.

I was right. There are no guards and no citizens here. And there is Julius, sitting at the top of the stairs again. As soon as he sees me and who I am with, he straightens up on his throne and slowly rises.

I stare at him for the first time since discovering the truth and feel something shift within me. Until now, I have felt nothing but a strong determination to unveil the truth and save the citizens from a manipulative, dangerous leader in order to ensure their safety. Now, seeing Julius's face, something powerful rises up and burns inside me that could explode if I don't carefully reel it in.

I have not heard a single word from Marquis since last night. Suddenly, I recognize his voice, gruffer than I've heard it so far.

"Get out," he snarls behind me.

There is a brief pause, and I am uncertain who Marquis is referring to until I see Julius nod to Steven behind us. A few moments later, the massive doors close as he exits.

Chapter 18

The burning sensation intensifies until I feel myself fuming. This man who I knew—who I trusted—tried to *kill* me. He manipulated me and *every other* citizen in this community into believing that he is a caring leader after stealing the crown from the rightful heir and even killing his own father. He's not a Ruler. He's a *monster*.

Before I know it, I begin to march forward with an involuntary growl, when Marquis's arm suddenly cuts in front of me like an iron barrier, blocking me from advancing.

"Let me handle this," Marquis says.

Julius is descending the stairs behind him. "Brother," he announces grandly with wide-open arms like he has missed the man that he cast out—along with his own father. "It's been so long. I'm surprised to see you've come back."

Marquis turns to him. "Brother," he acknowledges as he crosses the room to Julius. I follow his lead, remaining behind him, though I really don't want to.

"Come to challenge me again?" Julius says, almost like a joke. "Or have you come to attend our Commander's induction ceremony?"

He speaks with a taunting, arrogant air that I've never heard from Julius before. If there was any doubt regarding the truth, it's gone with just the few sentences that Julius has already spoken. He taunts Marquis in a way I previously never would have imagined, clearly aware that he's in a room full of individuals who already know the truth.

"I've come to tell you to—" Marquis looks down, and I worry that he has suddenly lost his nerve. "I've come to tell you I want you to continue your reign in peace," he says, leaving me in a state of shock. "You can remain as the Ruler of this community. Daia is to remain as Commander of the Forces, and she will do so respectfully while keeping your little secret. But don't you *ever* trick or deceive anyone like this again. You tried to get

Daia killed—just like you did your own father. I stood by and watched you do that because I was too young to know any better. I'm not going to stand around and watch you do this to anyone else. The Frozen Tundra is *not survivable* for people of mixed descent. You know that."

Marquis takes a step closer to Julius and raises a pointed finger. "But make no mistake, brother. If I ever catch you doing anything like this again, I will come back, and I will expose you for what you really are. I *will* expose the truth. I promise you that. And I have the blood to prove it. You want to challenge me for the crown?" He jerks his head to the massive doors behind us. "Let's both go out there and put ourselves to the test. Nobody has to believe me. We don't even have to fight for the crown. The people just need their eyes to see who lives and who dies out there— who ends up like me, and who ends up like your poor father, who was victimized by your selfish ego and cowardice."

Marquis practically hisses his words with disgust, which leads me to truly believe that he's not afraid of his brother. But I don't understand why he's backing down from the plan that we discussed last night.

Marquis turns to me and starts to walk me out.

"How do you know I won't just kill you?" Julius challenges. "I could send any of my soldiers to apprehend you at any time."

Marquis whips around so fast I feel a gust of wind. "I told you …" he snarls.

I turn around to see him rapidly marching up to Julius with a threatening finger pointed so intently at him that it scares me.

"Cowardice," Marquis spits. "You *reek* of it."

He comes to a halt almost nose to nose with Julius, and the slightly shorter, stockier build of our tribal ancestors is more apparent in Marquis than it is in Julius. For the first time, Julius barely even looks like a direct descendant to me.

"Now, you do wrong by any of these people again, and I will personally dethrone you. You can send whoever you want after me, but once they hear a sliver of the truth and find out the evidence can be so easily tested, you *know* there will be *nothing* left for you here."

Marquis stays there for a moment longer, Julius desperately trying to hold Marquis's gaze steadily without caving in.

Marquis eventually lets his gaze go and slowly turns to walk out with me following his lead.

Chapter 19

We exit through the doors. Steven still stands there, clearly confused by our impromptu visit.

I wait until we have distanced ourselves from the throne room before I say anything. "Why did you do that?"

Marquis looks at me.

"Why did you let him get away with it?"

"I didn't," he says.

I know that he threatened Julius, and I don't doubt that he would make good on every threat that he made in there. But I want to know why he gave in. The idea was to come here and set things right.

Marquis sighs, picking up on my dissatisfaction with how the situation was handled. "If

I dethroned him and took back the crown, look at all the turmoil the citizens of Taliver would have to go through."

I hadn't even thought about that. The citizens would be distraught. All these years, they thought they have been following someone with integrity, while a scandal happened right underneath their noses. A citizen was cast out to his death, and no one even knew. On top of which, the same citizen walked out the front gate with the heir to the crown, and no one realized it. Not to mention the disheartening fact that the tradition of pure tribal ancestry on the throne has been tainted.

Frankly, the list of disappointments and betrayals just goes on and on. Worst of all is probably the tainted bloodline wearing the crown, because that is a violation of the sacred agreement established between our tribal and native ancestors. The ensuing pain and distrust could be catastrophic for the citizens of Taliver. And would they even have confidence in a new Ruler? Though he's from this community, Marquis has not been a part of it for many years. He is basically a stranger to its citizens.

Clearly, my thoughts are visible on my face, because Marquis looks at me and says, "Exactly.

I don't want to put everyone through that. But you're right. These are my people. So, they are my responsibility. But I will not rule them by swooping in to create an uproar for them if I can avoid it. I will simply watch from nearby."

"But it'll all remain a lie," I tell him.

He takes a deep breath. "Daia, let me tell you something that I learned from my father when I was very small. We must pick our battles. Not everything that is a problem is meant to be dealt with how we think it should be. Sometimes, we have to take what we're given and make the best decision. That's what I'm doing: making the best decision for my people as their rightful Ruler."

What does one say to that?

"Don't you have a ceremony to get ready for?" Marquis asks.

Evidently, the induction ceremony is still taking place today. Julius must have planned to announce my absence during the ceremony, which means only Julius, Petrus, and whoever they might have told will be under the impression that I am missing. Marquis made it clear to Julius that I am to continue my duties in peace. And given Marquis's threats, there's nothing that

Julius can do about it. That being said, I need to tend to my duties for the ceremony. There is something else on my agenda, though.

"Yeah," I say. "I suppose I do, but I need to see the Seer first."

Marquis nods, and I lead the way to the study, expecting to find the Seer. Sure enough, there he is, sitting at the table I sat at just a few days ago. Something bright bursts inside of me—happiness. I'm so happy to see him—free from any threat of being exiled. There were times I thought I'd never see him again.

I knock on the open door. He turns around, and his entire countenance brightens. He immediately gets up, charges for me, and wraps me in a warm embrace. There has been so much going on I haven't really had the headspace to hear myself think. Seeing the Seer, though, instills a sense of levelheadedness that I didn't realize I was missing and gives me some element of normality that makes me truly feel back at home.

He eventually lets me go and holds me at arm's length to examine me.

"How are you? I thought you were *dead*." His voice chokes slightly on the last word, a tear welling in his eye.

I shake my head. "No, I'm not dead. Far from it. Is that what the Ruler told you?"

He nods. "Yes. He was going to make an announcement at your induction ceremony. What happened? How are you here right now?"

"He helped me," I explain, looking at Marquis.

The Seer follows my gaze.

"This … is Marquis."

The Seer looks at Marquis with gratitude in his eyes as he extends his hand to shake Marquis's.

"He's the rightful Ruler," I tell him.

The Seer freezes in the middle of shaking Marquis's hand and glances at me in confusion. He looks back at Marquis, and, to my surprise, his countenance softens almost into an expression of amusement.

"Of course," the Seer says to himself. "The prior Seer's son."

I look at him in surprise. He knows. He must have somehow already suspected the current Ruler's false identity.

The Seer looks at me. "The old Seer … I was aware that he had a son, and I used to see him sometimes while his father was still a part of the community. Then, after the Seer left Taliver, I never saw his son again—not even when I visited. It was as if he had just vanished. I always just assumed he was still in the community somewhere, staying with family. I never would have imagined that he somehow stole the crown." He looks at Marquis. "Where have you been all this time?"

"In the Tundra," Marquis says.

The Seer bites his lip and nods. "I figured as much."

The Seer looks at me. "Daia, what exactly happened out there?"

I take a deep breath, and then I tell him about Julius manipulating me into following him the other night, about the threat to exile the Seer, about Julius's willingness to remove people he feels are a threat to his reign, about the death sentence placed on me and the truth behind his predecessor's death ... I tell him everything.

The Seer stares off into space, shaking his head, his arms crossed. "I can't believe that the Ruler would go so far," he says. "There were always questionable behaviors that didn't line up with those of a descendant of our tribal ancestors, but murder? Manipulation? To be so insensitive to the needs and well-being of your people ... This has to be made right."

There's no question where my fire for justice comes from.

Marquis jumps in. "Not at the risk of the well-being of the citizens."

The Seer looks at Marquis incredulously. "They *are* at risk—under the rule of someone as dangerous as their current Ruler."

"I'm not going to divide Taliver into a civil war or a revolution that could cost people their lives."

They go on and on, back and forth, and I realize that I'm the only one left to consider the situation from an objective standpoint, and my induction ceremony should be starting very soon. My induction ceremony, where I'm supposed to speak—where I will make whatever announcements that I deem fit for my people as I become Commander of the Forces.

It's amazing how just a few days ago, I was so worried about the speech—whether people would understand and relate to it, whether it would inspire soldiers to confidently follow me as their leader or discourage them from doing so, and just how well I can fill the shoes of my predecessors.

Now I hardly care. I realize that the speech is about more than just making a statement. It's a part of my role as Commander, protecting my citizens. Achieving admiration for the speech from the citizens of Taliver is insignificant. What *is* significant is whose hands the citizens are left in and fulfilling my duty. I agree with Marquis's intention to protect the citizens from uproar, but I also agree with the Seer—nothing is worth the citizens' lives being jeopardized in the hands of a manipulative murderer.

Chapter 20

I stand on an elevated stage in the courtyard, where the Ruler makes announcements and where pretty much every official matter takes place. I'm at the podium, my hands braced on the wooden edges as I stare out at the numerous bodies of shining armor situated in rows before me, awaiting the commencement of my induction ceremony.

Red flags marked with a golden crown and bordered in gold are scattered throughout the gathering. They're on select suits of armor, and they tower above the assembly as banners. I imagine Petrus out there somewhere, surprised and likely confused by my presence— as is anyone else that he might have told I was gone.

In the distance, behind the soldiers in front of me, is a large fountain with a female statue gracefully reaching out in dance as though earnestly longing for something. Water spouts out of her extended fingertips, her pointed toes on a raised foot, and her mouth as though she sings an aquatic melody.

On either side of the soldiers in front of me, in large stands and balconies scaling the towering gray buildings bordering the courtyard, are other citizens—those who can fit here, anyway. The others spread out beyond the fountain or listen from within the buildings. The buildings on either side run into the one towering behind me. The only way out of this courtyard is straight ahead by the fountain, with the exception of going through the buildings.

Julius is positioned to the side of the stage with his crown and his scepter again, guarded by a couple of soldiers as usual. He just stands there, unable to do anything to stop this ceremony.

It didn't take me long to jot down a few key points for my speech before coming out here.

1. Gratitude
2. Intentions for the forces
3. Desire for Taliver

That's basically it. I wanted to express my appreciation for the honorable role being bestowed on me, and I wanted to set a vision for the soldiers and for the citizens of Taliver—one of protection and integrity, which is no different from the vision set by my predecessors before me. But I wanted to make the commitment from me personally. I was going to emphasize the kind of community we want to be without explicitly addressing the scandals or anything else that could create a panic. However, though the task of giving the speech doesn't weigh on me as much as it used to, something still doesn't feel right.

Looking down at my general notes, I don't feel that this is what I need to say to the people. They need to know who I truly am— who is truly leading the forces. So, I need to be honest and to *protect* them from any dangerous threats—even threats of falsehood from within Taliver. That is my responsibility. It's my *duty*. Marquis recognized his responsibility and has decided what battles to fight. Now, I have to do the same.

"Citizens of Taliver!" I announce. "We are gathered here to witness our community grow and continue to evolve and flourish." I look up to address the people. "You have put your trust in Taliver, in our …"

I trail off. Their trust. They've put their trust in a lie.

I realize that I'm obstructing the flow of my speech. I can practically see the Seer and Marquis trying to understand what is wrong with me.

The Seer …

The Seer said he would travel into the Tundra all those years ago to see his predecessor. Yet, he *survived* … even though he is of mixed descent. Either there is more to his identity than he knows, or he is hiding something from me too. Subconsciously worried about what this could mean, I push the thought out of my mind. He wouldn't hide anything from me. He is not my enemy. Nonetheless, there are far too many lies plaguing this community. *They have to stop!*

I forget about the paper in my hands on the podium.

"You have put your trust in our governing body and are loyal to the wellness of our community," I continue. "But you have been following a lie!"

The assembly erupts into low utterances of surprise that reverberate throughout the courtyard. I look over at Marquis and the Seer to my left, standing on the far side by a bordering building with flabbergasted expressions.

I glance at the other side of the stage. Julius stands there, looking more angry than surprised, but I don't care. I will restore our community, and I *will* protect its citizens—even from him. There's nothing that he can do. He can try to stop me. He can apprehend me and call me a liar. He can cast me out into the Tundra fifty times. It doesn't matter, because right now, if I know nothing else, I know this: I will *never* stop fighting for my people.

AUTHOR'S NOTE

Thank you for reading *The Blizzard's Secrets*! After the long hours of writing, numerous rounds of editing, and tireless revisions, your readership means so much to me. It takes a lot of time and effort to share these stories with people, but it is totally worth it. I love the highs and lows in an exciting, suspenseful tale, and being able to create the adventure of a roller-coaster story for others to enjoy is a treasured experience for me.

Something else that means the world to me is hearing from the most important people to my books: you, the reader. Your voice is powerful, and a review from you would mean so much to me and my books. Reviews help spread the word about *The Blizzard's Secrets* to other readers. They also help me truly know your experience reading my books—what stood out to you, what you loved, what your favorite parts and characters are,and what you look forward to.

You can leave an honest review and find **bonus content** about *The Blizzard's Secrets* at the link below or by scanning the QR code.

theblizzardssecrets.com/bonus-content

I look forward to hearing from you!

And watch out for more stories coming your way!

Enjoyed
The Blizzard's Secrets?

Scan for more about the world
of Taliver, your favorite
characters, and other bonus
features and special gifts!

ABOUT THE AUTHOR

DJanée is an author and a poet. As a poet, she writes about various topics pertaining to life and the world we live in. As an author, she writes material ranging from children's books to young adult fiction.

With a collection of children's books, short stories, and poems to her name, DJanée is a multifaceted writer of various genres and formats. Her published books include *Jimmy and the Teddy Bear*, *The Blizzard's Secrets*, and *On the Run*, the first book in the young adult dystopian series *More Than Conquerors*.

DJanée uses her works to captivate, inspire, encourage, and entertain. When she is not writing poetry or stories, she is learning something new, such as a new language, a new skill, or random facts. She also enjoys traveling with loved ones.

You can visit her website at
www.djaneecreations.com.

Facebook, Instagram,
Pinterest: @djaneecreations.

www.ingramcontent.com/pod-product-compliance
Lightning Source LLC
Chambersburg PA
CBHW020118310726
48970CB00002B/688